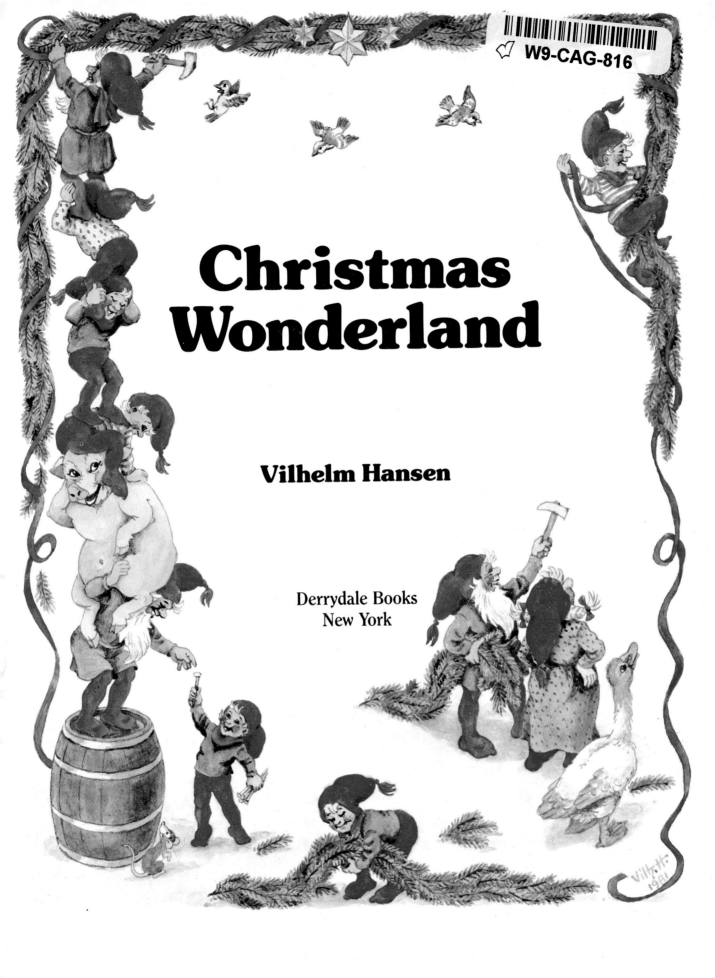

Christmas Wonderland

Vilhelm Hansen

Derrydale Books
New York

W9-CAG-816

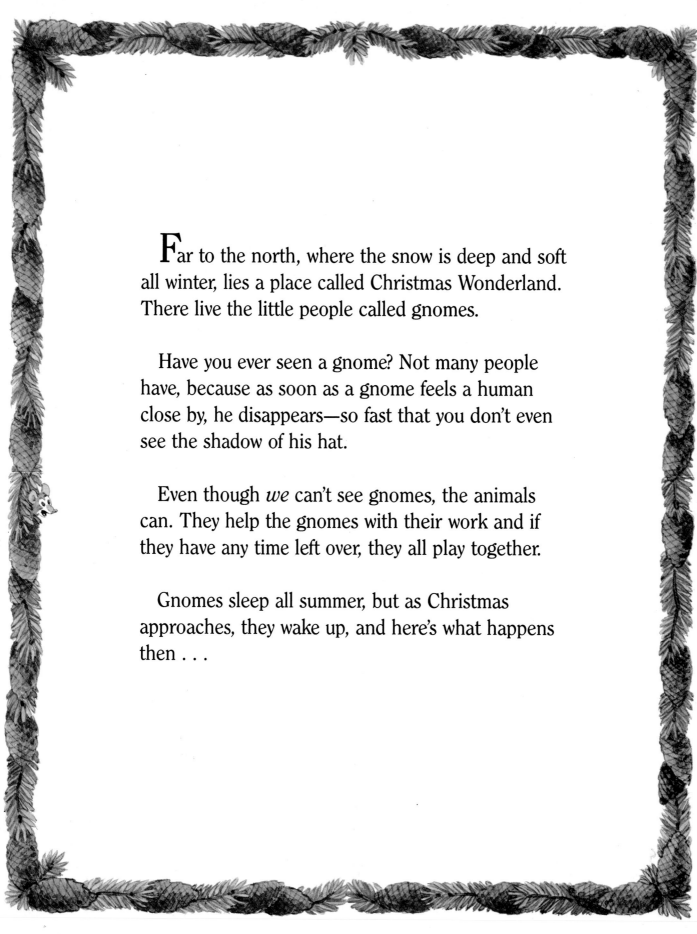

Far to the north, where the snow is deep and soft all winter, lies a place called Christmas Wonderland. There live the little people called gnomes.

Have you ever seen a gnome? Not many people have, because as soon as a gnome feels a human close by, he disappears—so fast that you don't even see the shadow of his hat.

Even though *we* can't see gnomes, the animals can. They help the gnomes with their work and if they have any time left over, they all play together.

Gnomes sleep all summer, but as Christmas approaches, they wake up, and here's what happens then . . .

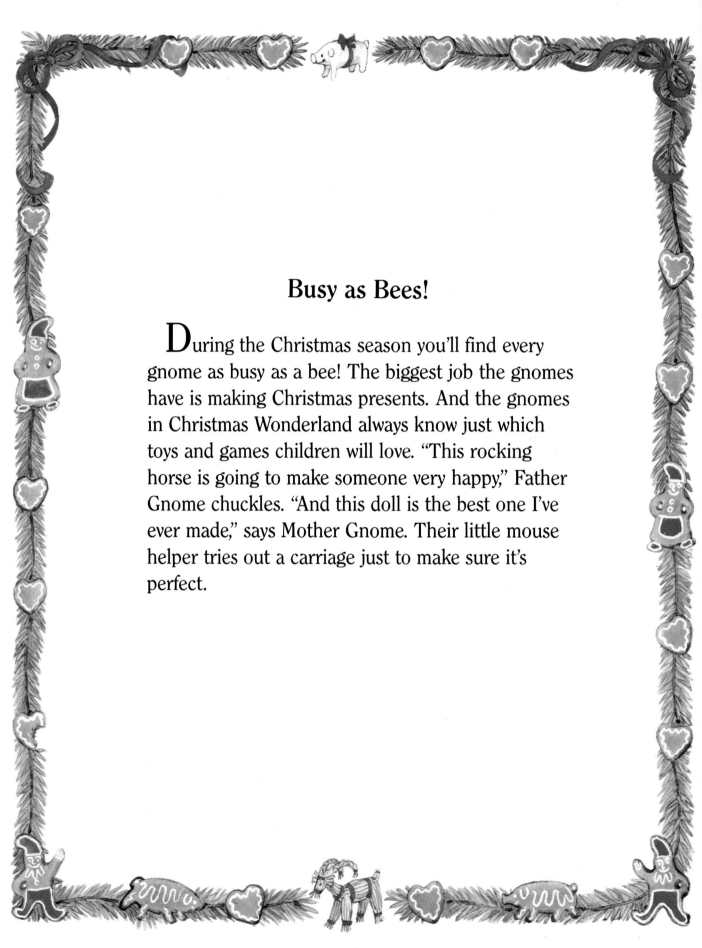

Busy as Bees!

During the Christmas season you'll find every gnome as busy as a bee! The biggest job the gnomes have is making Christmas presents. And the gnomes in Christmas Wonderland always know just which toys and games children will love. "This rocking horse is going to make someone very happy," Father Gnome chuckles. "And this doll is the best one I've ever made," says Mother Gnome. Their little mouse helper tries out a carriage just to make sure it's perfect.

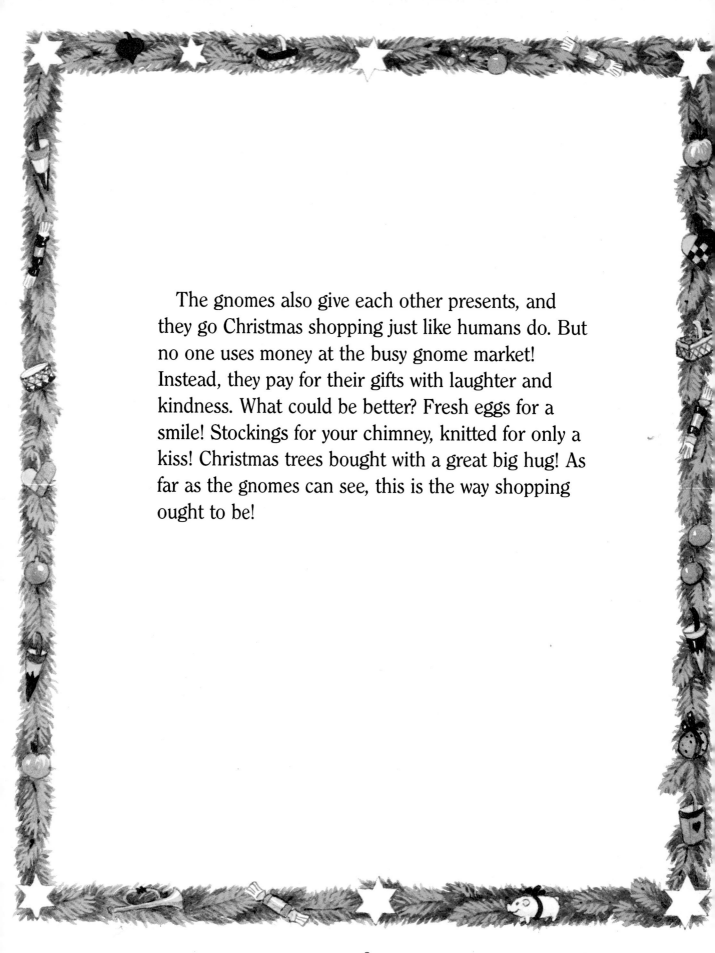

The gnomes also give each other presents, and they go Christmas shopping just like humans do. But no one uses money at the busy gnome market! Instead, they pay for their gifts with laughter and kindness. What could be better? Fresh eggs for a smile! Stockings for your chimney, knitted for only a kiss! Christmas trees bought with a great big hug! As far as the gnomes can see, this is the way shopping ought to be!

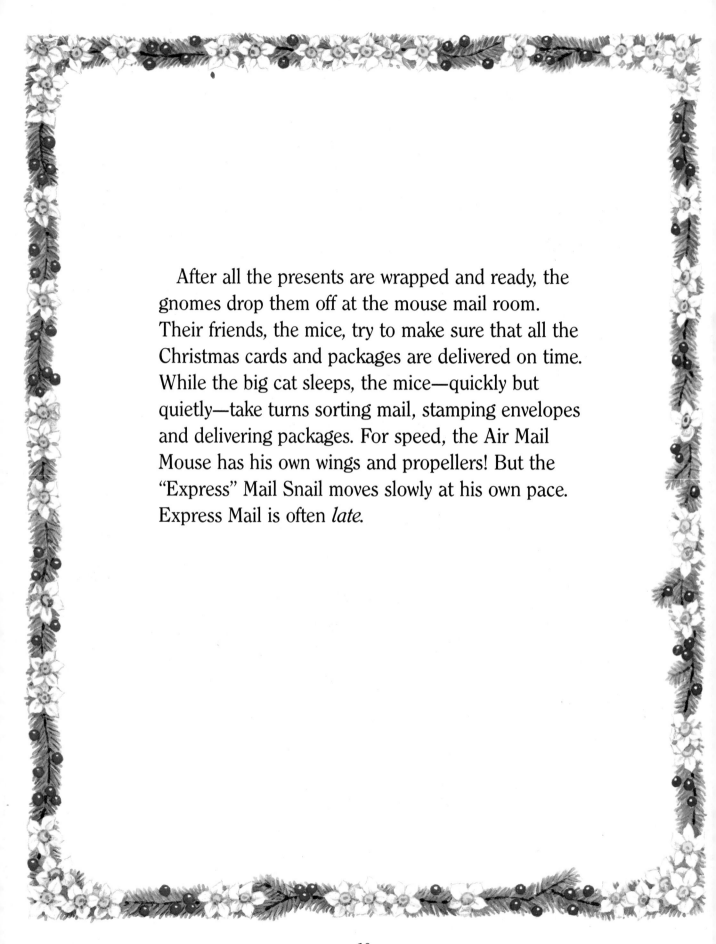

After all the presents are wrapped and ready, the gnomes drop them off at the mouse mail room. Their friends, the mice, try to make sure that all the Christmas cards and packages are delivered on time. While the big cat sleeps, the mice—quickly but quietly—take turns sorting mail, stamping envelopes and delivering packages. For speed, the Air Mail Mouse has his own wings and propellers! But the "Express" Mail Snail moves slowly at his own pace. Express Mail is often *late*.

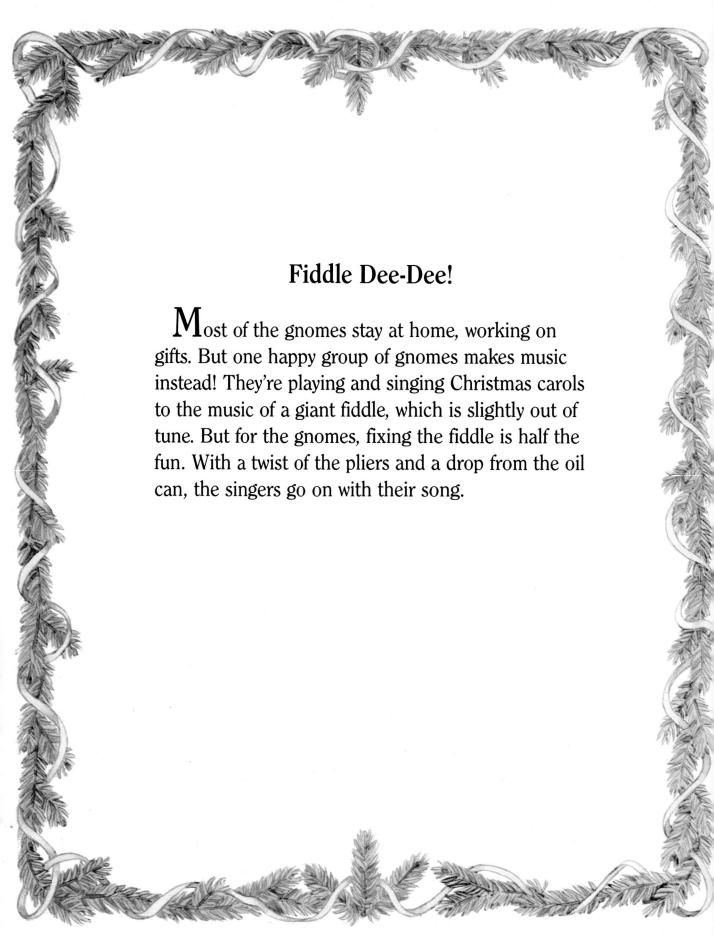

Fiddle Dee-Dee!

Most of the gnomes stay at home, working on gifts. But one happy group of gnomes makes music instead! They're playing and singing Christmas carols to the music of a giant fiddle, which is slightly out of tune. But for the gnomes, fixing the fiddle is half the fun. With a twist of the pliers and a drop from the oil can, the singers go on with their song.

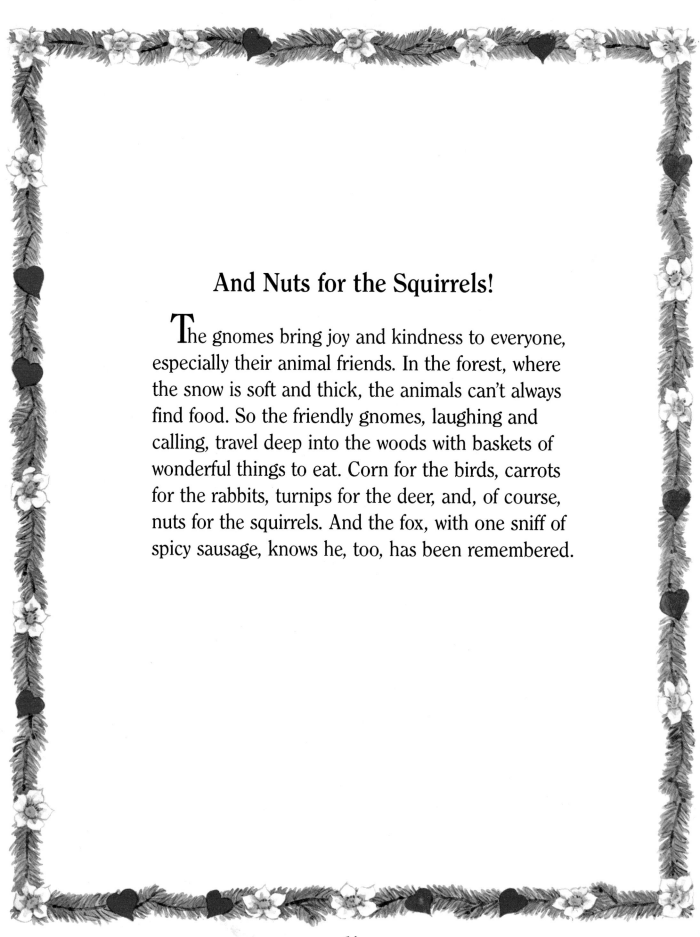

And Nuts for the Squirrels!

The gnomes bring joy and kindness to everyone, especially their animal friends. In the forest, where the snow is soft and thick, the animals can't always find food. So the friendly gnomes, laughing and calling, travel deep into the woods with baskets of wonderful things to eat. Corn for the birds, carrots for the rabbits, turnips for the deer, and, of course, nuts for the squirrels. And the fox, with one sniff of spicy sausage, knows he, too, has been remembered.

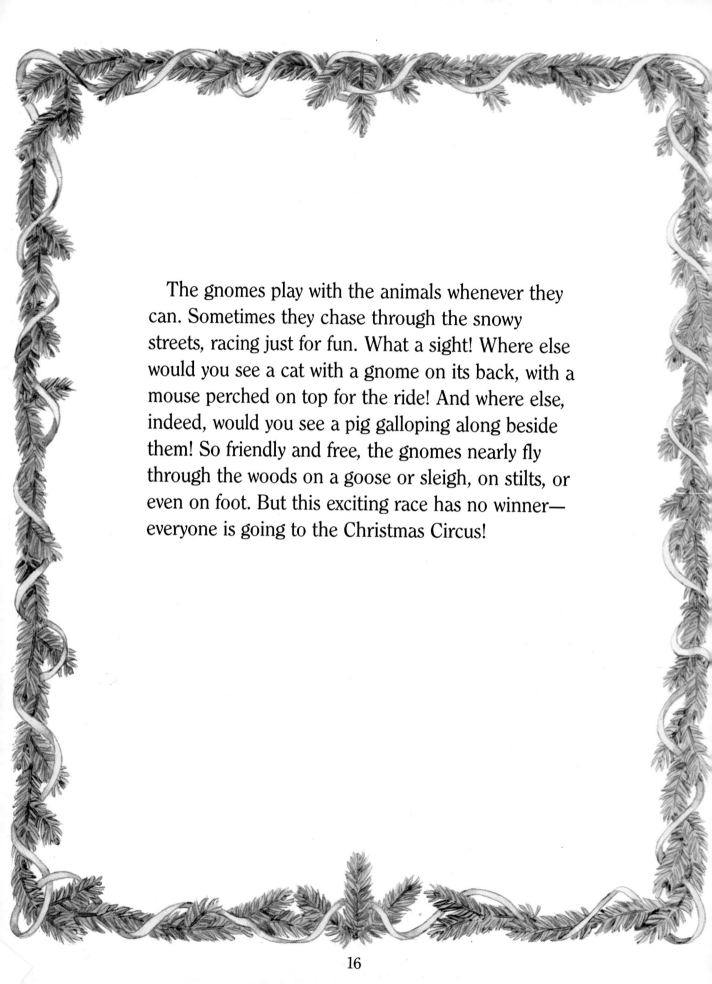

The gnomes play with the animals whenever they can. Sometimes they chase through the snowy streets, racing just for fun. What a sight! Where else would you see a cat with a gnome on its back, with a mouse perched on top for the ride! And where else, indeed, would you see a pig galloping along beside them! So friendly and free, the gnomes nearly fly through the woods on a goose or sleigh, on stilts, or even on foot. But this exciting race has no winner—everyone is going to the Christmas Circus!

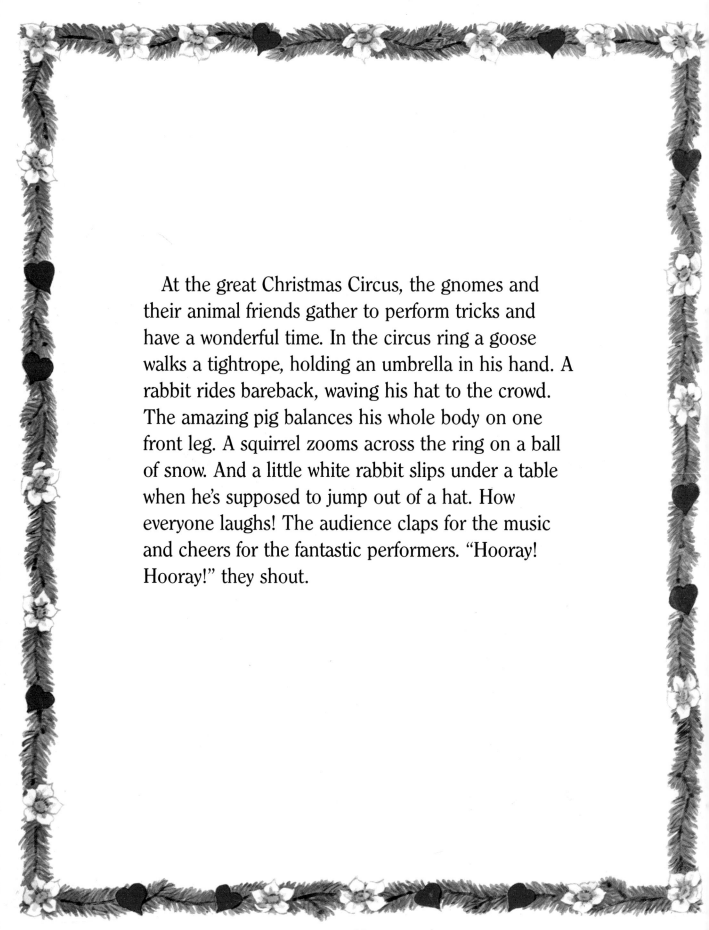

At the great Christmas Circus, the gnomes and
their animal friends gather to perform tricks and
have a wonderful time. In the circus ring a goose
walks a tightrope, holding an umbrella in his hand. A
rabbit rides bareback, waving his hat to the crowd.
The amazing pig balances his whole body on one
front leg. A squirrel zooms across the ring on a ball
of snow. And a little white rabbit slips under a table
when he's supposed to jump out of a hat. How
everyone laughs! The audience claps for the music
and cheers for the fantastic performers. "Hooray!
Hooray!" they shout.

So Many Cookies!

Christmas baking in the land of gnomes is a grand occasion. They start from scratch with flour the miller gnome has milled especially for Christmas. When they pull the flour home on a sled, all their animal friends gather around, for they know that where there's flour, there will soon be cookies. Butter and flour, sugar and spice, are mixed together and rolled into a delicious dough. Busy gnomes cut out gingerbread people and hearts. There are so many cookies! They look so good coming out of the oven and smell even better. How can anyone wait until Christmas?

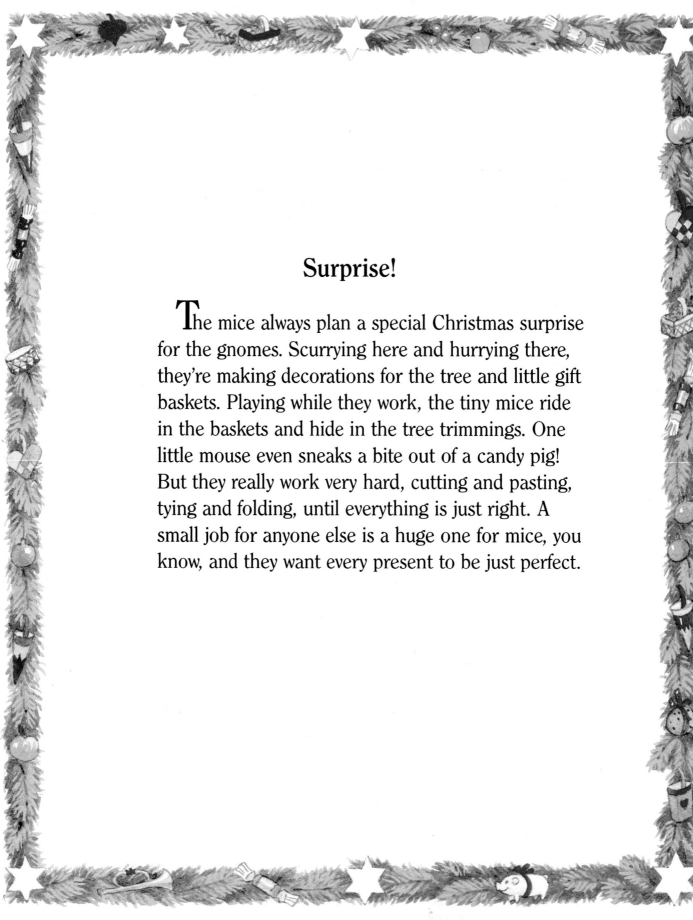

Surprise!

The mice always plan a special Christmas surprise for the gnomes. Scurrying here and hurrying there, they're making decorations for the tree and little gift baskets. Playing while they work, the tiny mice ride in the baskets and hide in the tree trimmings. One little mouse even sneaks a bite out of a candy pig! But they really work very hard, cutting and pasting, tying and folding, until everything is just right. A small job for anyone else is a huge one for mice, you know, and they want every present to be just perfect.

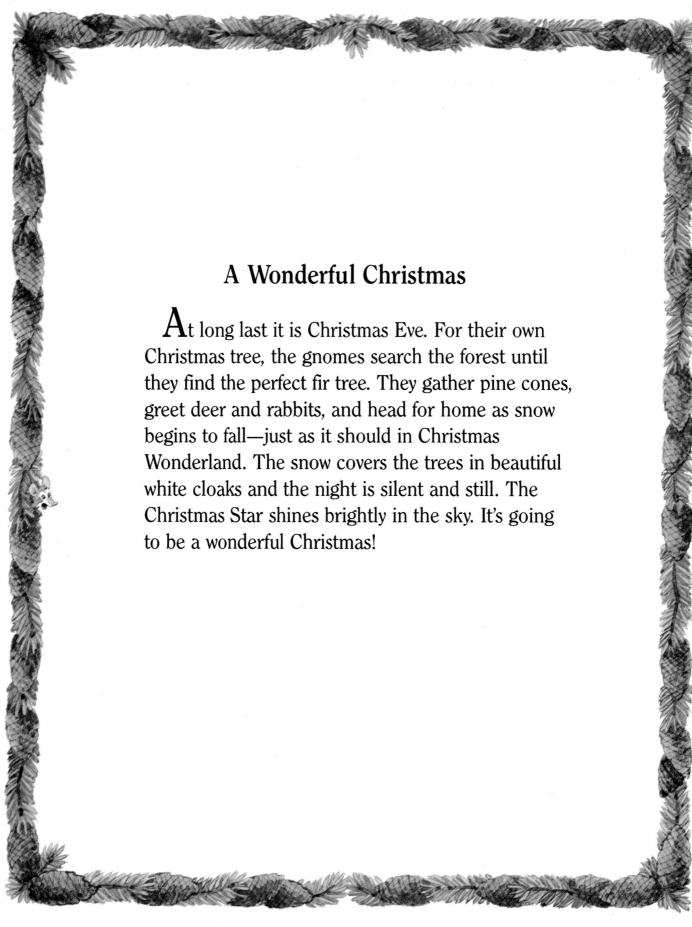

A Wonderful Christmas

At long last it is Christmas Eve. For their own Christmas tree, the gnomes search the forest until they find the perfect fir tree. They gather pine cones, greet deer and rabbits, and head for home as snow begins to fall—just as it should in Christmas Wonderland. The snow covers the trees in beautiful white cloaks and the night is silent and still. The Christmas Star shines brightly in the sky. It's going to be a wonderful Christmas!

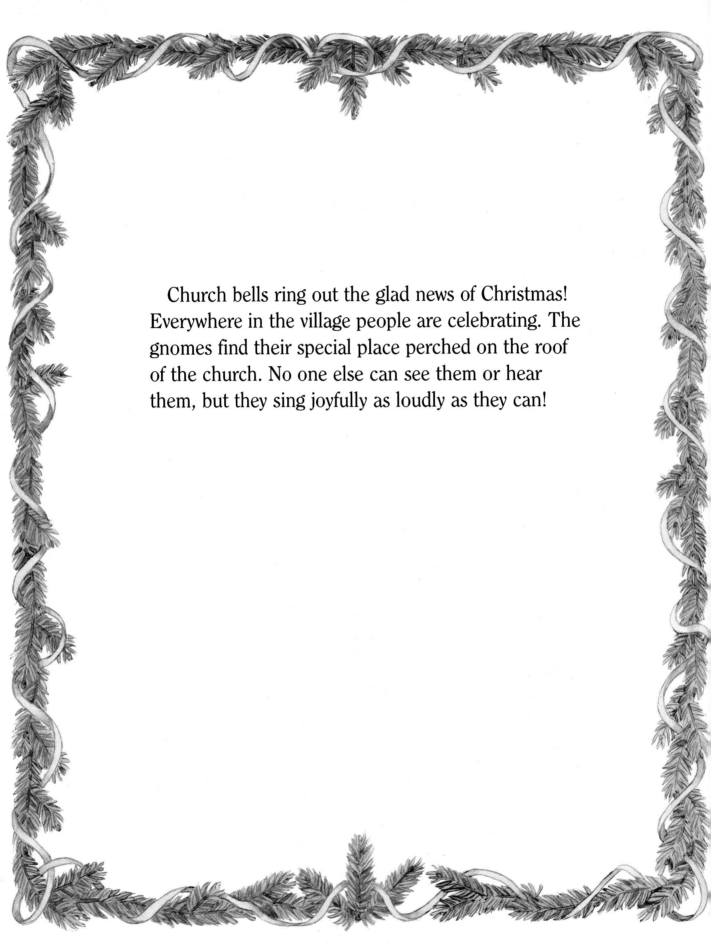

Church bells ring out the glad news of Christmas! Everywhere in the village people are celebrating. The gnomes find their special place perched on the roof of the church. No one else can see them or hear them, but they sing joyfully as loudly as they can!

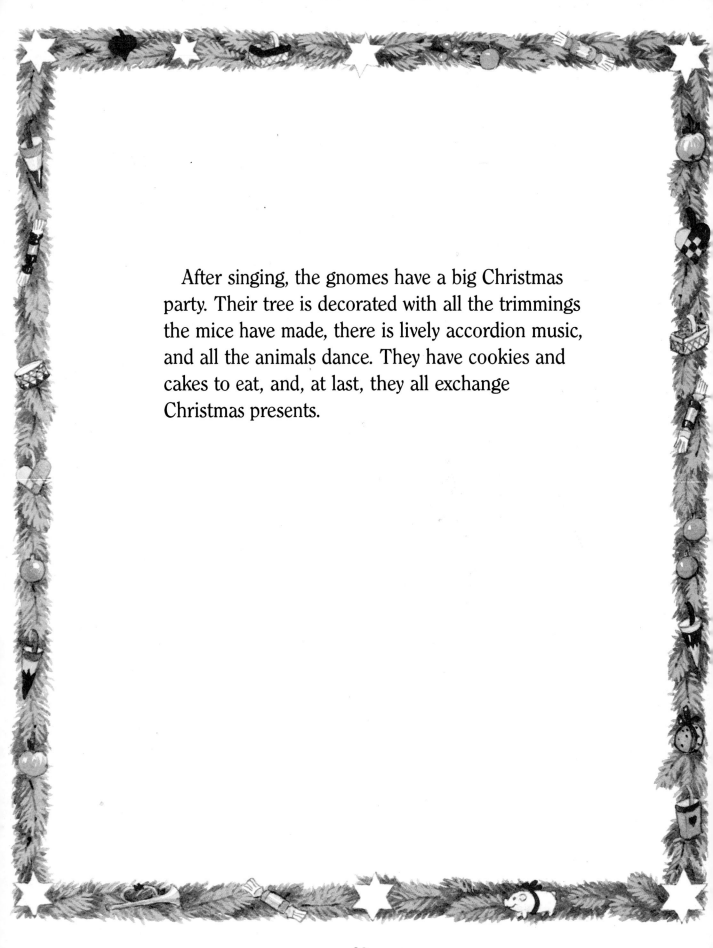

After singing, the gnomes have a big Christmas party. Their tree is decorated with all the trimmings the mice have made, there is lively accordion music, and all the animals dance. They have cookies and cakes to eat, and, at last, they all exchange Christmas presents.

Later, at the gnome village, a merry bell rings outside. The Gnome King has arrived! Two little gnomes toss out presents for all the gnomes and animals. And then, the sleigh speeds swiftly away—for the Gnome King has more stops to make.

And now Christmas is over. With their work finally done, the gnomes go home. And they will sleep until the month before Christmas next year. Sometimes it does happen that a young gnome wakes up and feels like having a bit of fun. So don't be surprised if your hat flies off when there is no wind blowing. It might be a little gnome playing a trick on you. But he'll soon join the others again—to sleep and dream about next Christmas in Wonderland!